Smithsonian Prehistoric Zone

Velociraptor

by Gerry Bailey
Illustrated by Karen Carr

Crabtree Publishing Company

www.crabtreebooks.com

Crabtree Publishing Company

www.crabtreebooks.com

Author
Gerry Bailey

Illustrator
Karen Carr

Editorial coordinator
Kathy Middleton

Editor
Lynn Peppas

Proofreader
Kathy Middleton

Prepress technician
Samara Parent

Print and production coordinator
Katherine Berti

Library of Congress Cataloging-in-Publication Data

Bailey, Gerry.
  Velociraptor / by Gerry Bailey ; illustrated by Karen Carr.
    p. cm. -- (Smithsonian prehistoric zone)
  Includes index.
  ISBN 978-0-7787-1820-8 (pbk. : alk. paper) -- ISBN 978-0-7787-1807-9
(reinforced library binding : alk. paper) -- ISBN 978-1-4271-9711-5
(electronic (pdf))
  1. Velociraptor--Juvenile literature. I. Carr, Karen, 1960- , ill. II. Title.

QE862.S3B347 2011
567.912--dc22
                        2010044036

Library and Archives Canada Cataloguing in Publication

Bailey, Gerry
    Velociraptor / by Gerry Bailey ; illustrated by Karen Carr.

(Smithsonian prehistoric zone)
Includes index.
At head of title: Smithsonian Institution.
Issued also in electronic format.
ISBN 978-0-7787-1807-9 (bound).--ISBN 978-0-7787-1820-8 (pbk.)

    1. Velociraptor--Juvenile literature. I. Carr, Karen, 1960-
II. Smithsonian Institution III. Title. IV. Series: Bailey, Gerry.
Smithsonian prehistoric zone.

QE862.S3B339 2011   j567.912   C2010-906898-X

Crabtree Publishing Company

www.crabtreebooks.com   1-800-387-7650
Copyright © **2011 CRABTREE PUBLISHING COMPANY**.

Published in the United States
Crabtree Publishing
PMB 59051
350 Fifth Avenue, 59th Floor
New York, New York 10118

Published in Canada
Crabtree Publishing
616 Welland Ave.
St. Catharines, Ontario
L2M 5V6

Printed in China/012011/GW20101014

Dinosaurs

Living things had been around for billions of years before dinosaurs **evolved**. Animal life on Earth started with single-cell **organisms** that lived in the seas. About 380 million years ago, some animals came out of the sea and onto land. These were the ancestors that would become the mighty dinosaurs.

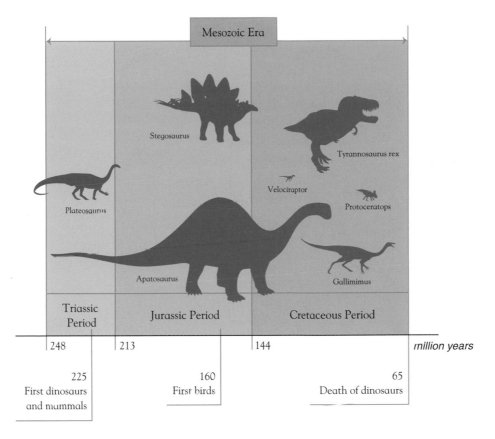

Mesozoic Era

Stegosaurus

Tyrannosaurus rex

Velociraptor

Protoceratops

Plateosaurus

Apatosaurus

Gallimimus

Triassic Period	Jurassic Period	Cretaceous Period

248   213   144   *million years*

225
First dinosaurs
and mammals

160
First birds

65
Death of dinosaurs

The dinosaur era is called the Mesozoic era. It is divided into three parts called the Triassic, Jurassic, and Cretaceous periods. During the Cretaceous period flowering plants grew for the first time. Plant-eating dinosaurs, such as *Protoceratops*, lived. Meat-eaters, such as *Tyrannosaurus rex* and *Velociraptor*, fed on the plant-eaters and other dinosaurs. Some dinosaurs, such as *Gallimimus*, were **omnivores**. This meant they ate plants and meat. By the end of the Cretaceous period, dinosaurs (except for birds) had been wiped out. No one is exactly sure why.

4

It was very still and quiet. It was also fiercely hot. The Sun that beat down 75 million years ago was far warmer than we know it today.

From behind a rock a hand appeared. It had long fingers and sharp, deadly claws. Another limb slowly followed. Then a scaly, feathered head appeared with wide-open eyes. It glanced this way and that along the valley that stretched below.

The creature sprang to the top of the rocky ridge to get a better view of the valley. It looked like a bird but it was not. It was a deadly Velociraptor. This 50 pound (22 kilogram) dinosaur was terrifying. The beast stood only three feet (1 meter) tall on two legs. It was fast, smart, and ferocious.

Velociraptor was looking for the rest of his pack.
And there they were, just below him. Velociraptor
set off to join them. Over many thousands of years,

these intelligent dinosaurs had learned that it was easier to hunt in packs than on their own. The pack set off in search of food.

The Velociraptors traveled fast across the flat
ground. They ran with their tails sticking out
behind them. It helped them to stay balanced.

They could turn quickly to **avoid** danger or if they caught sight of **prey**. Velociraptors were among the fastest of all dinosaurs.

Suddenly the Velociraptors spotted an ostrich-like dinosaur with a long neck and broad beak called Gallimimus. It was bigger than they were and could run much faster, but it would make a good meal if they could catch it. Working as a team the Velociraptors could easily **outwit** the Gallimimus.

Velociraptor and his pack searched
for more food after they had finished
their meal. Velociraptor spotted an
Oviraptor near a nest.

Oviraptor saw Velociraptor coming and knew she had better run. She knew she was no match for one Velociraptor, let alone a whole pack of them. The Velociraptors helped themselves to the eggs.

Now the pack was thirsty. They headed for a stream nearby. Other animals were already there drinking. They all shared the small amount of water available in the dry valley. The animals looked up as the pack raced toward the stream. They **recognized** the Velociraptors and scattered in all directions. They ran for their lives.

Velociraptor and his pack drank and moved on.
He heard the sounds of fighting in the distance.
The Oviraptor that had escaped from them was now
attacking a small dinosaur called a Protoceratops.

The pack rushed forward. They would chase off the winner and feast on the loser. The Oviraptor and Protoceratops saw them and fled. They did not want to fight while Velociraptors around.

Now it was time to rest. Velociraptor
lay down and flicked out his special
claw, which curved like a **sickle**.

These claws were his most fearsome
weapons. He had to take care of them.
He picked them clean, then slept.

Velociraptor was woken by the sound of
something shuffling about nearby. He bared
his sharp, pointed teeth. A tiny mammal
scurried past but Velociraptor was too quick.

24

He lashed out with his claws and trapped the animal. Then he let it go. He was not hungry, but he enjoyed practicing his hunting skills. After all, he was one of the most ferocious **predators** in the land.

All about Velociraptor

(vee-LOSS-ee-RAP-tor)

Velociraptor means "speedy thief." It lived around 75 million years ago during the late Cretaceous period. It lived in the area where China and Mongolia are today. The climate was hot and dry, and there were just a few streams.

Velociraptor was a lightweight dinosaur that weighed about 45 pounds (20 kg). It stood three feet (1 meter) tall and was about six feet (1.8 meters) long. It had long, slender legs and a stiff tail that it used for balance. It ran faster than most plant-eaters and used its tail to change direction quickly. This meant it was probably able to catch almost any small dinosaur it chased. *Velociraptor* killed the prey it caught with its razor-sharp claws. It had a special curved claw on the second toe of each foot that it could draw back when it ran. This claw was its main weapon.

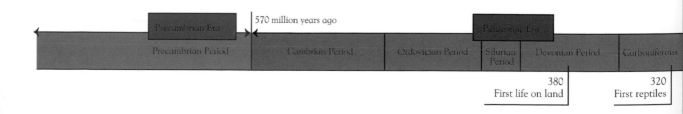

570 million years ago

| Precambrian Era | | | Paleozoic Era | | |
| Precambrian Period | Cambrian Period | Ordovician Period | Silurian Period | Devonian Period | Carboniferous |

380
First life on land

320
First reptiles

Velociraptor's head was long and low with a long snout. Another member of its family, called the *dromaeosaurs*, had the same head shape. *Velociraptor's* sharp, curved teeth were just under one inch (2.5 centimeters) long. They were good for tearing off chunks of meat.

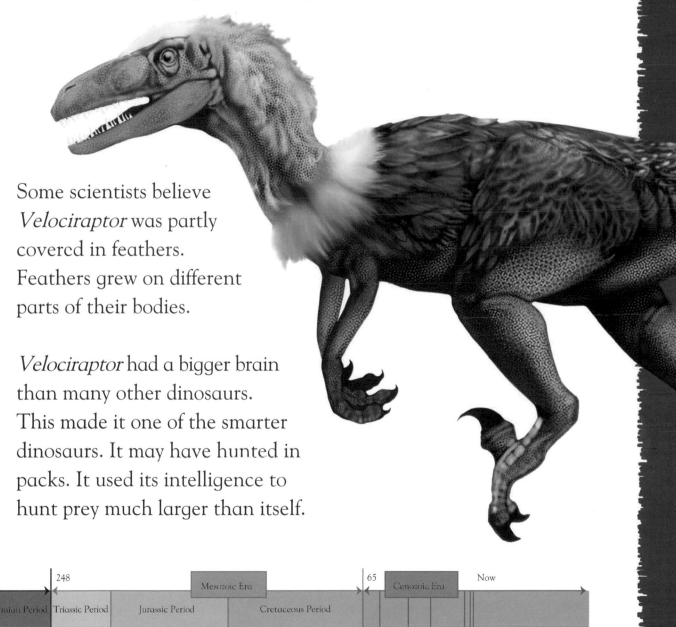

Some scientists believe *Velociraptor* was partly covered in feathers. Feathers grew on different parts of their bodies.

Velociraptor had a bigger brain than many other dinosaurs. This made it one of the smarter dinosaurs. It may have hunted in packs. It used its intelligence to hunt prey much larger than itself.

248

Mesozoic Era

65

Cenozoic Era

Now

Period | Permian Period | Triassic Period | Jurassic Period | Cretaceous Period

1.8
First humans

Tiny dinosaurs

When we think of dinosaurs we usually think of giant ones such as the fearsome *Tyrannosaurus rex* or the 85-foot-(26-meter) long *Diplodocus*. But not all dinosaurs were large. In fact some were quite small. *Velociraptor* was a ferocious predator, but it was only about six feet (1.8 meters) long—about as long as a male sheep.

Compsognathus was just 24–26 inches (60–65 centimeters) long. It was about the size of a chicken. It was hollow-boned and built for speed. This dinosaur lived during the late Jurassic period.

Sinosauropteryx lived in what is now China. It measured 4 feet (1.25 meters) in length. **Fossilized** stomach remains show that it

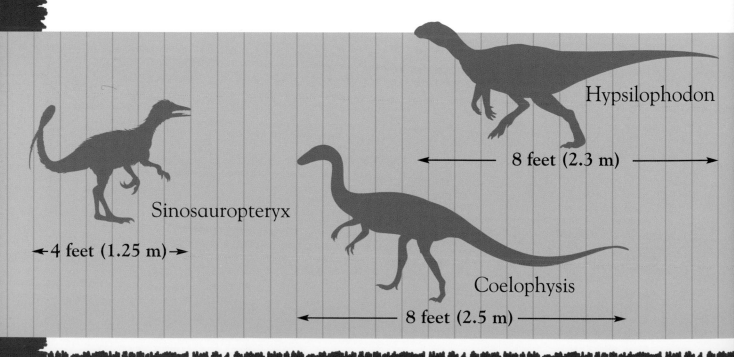

Hypsilophodon
8 feet (2.3 m)
Sinosauropteryx
4 feet (1.25 m)
Coelophysis
8 feet (2.5 m)

fed on lizards and small mammals. It's the first dinosaur fossil found to show marks that look like feathers.

Hypsilophodon lived in the early Cretaceous period. This little dinosaur was just five to eight feet (1.5–2.3 meters) long. It had tall, **grooved** cheek teeth that helped it to chew and grind tough plant food.

Coelophysis lived during the Triassic period. It was about eight to ten feet (2.5 meters) long. It used its strong, clawed hands to grab prey.

Troodon is a dinosaur that used to be called *Stenonychosaurus*. It was just eight to ten feet (2.3–3 meters) long. Scientists think it was the most intelligent dinosaur. Its brain, when compared to its bodysize, is the largest discovered so far. In the world of dinosaurs being small did not mean that you were not smart!

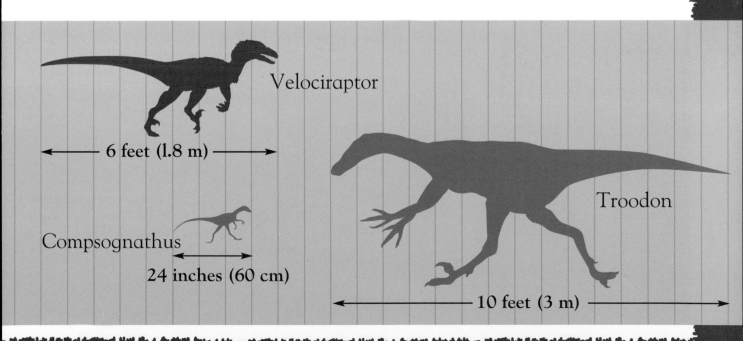

Velociraptor

← 6 feet (1.8 m) →

Compsognathus

← 24 inches (60 cm) →

Troodon

← 10 feet (3 m) →

Different feet for different lives

Dinosaurs had different kinds of feet to suit their lifestyles. For example, an *Apatosaurus* had short, broad feet much like an elephant's today. They were designed to help support the plant-eating animal's great weight.

Small, fast-moving dinosaurs, such as *Velociraptor*, had slim feet with sharp, pointed claws on each finger and toe. The second toe had a spectacular curved claw that acted like a sickle. The claws on its hands were probably used to hold on to its prey. Its sickle-like back claw was used to slash it to pieces.

Apatosaurus had wide sturdy feet that helped support its huge body.

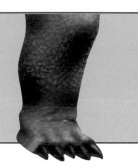

Tyrannosaurus rex had three large claws on its toes, with a small one behind the foot.

Velociraptor had sharp, clawed feet with a sickle-like claw on the second toe.

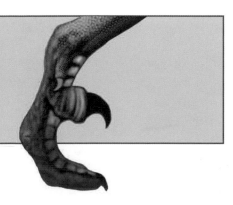

Glossary

agile Having the ability to move quickly

avoid To stay away from

evolve To change and grow over time

fossilized The hardening of remains of an organism that lived thousands of years ago

groove A narrow channel or trench

omnivore An animal that eats both plants and animals

organism Any living plant or animal

outwit To be smarter than

predator An animal that hunts other animals for food

prey An animal that is hunted by another

recognize To know what something is

sickle A sharp, knife-like object with an outwardly rounded blade

Index

Further Reading and Websites

Velociraptor Up Close: Swift Dinosaur by Peter Dodson. Enslow Elementary (2010)

Velociraptor and Other Raptors and Small Carnivores by David West. Gareth Stevens Publishing (2010)

Websites:

www.smithsonianeducation.org